CHAI AUR KAHANI

HAPPILY EVER AFTER IS NOT A FAIRYTALE, ITS A CHOICE

MIHIR BOMMISETTY

Made with ♥ on the Notion Press Platform
www.notionpress.com

To the love that left me through my life, yet left its imprint on my soul,
To my family, whose unwavering support held me through the storm,
And to my best friends, the ones who turned heartache into healing with their laughter and light,

To the dreamers who carry untold stories in their hearts,
To the ones who dare to love fiercely, despite the pain.

Contents

Contents

Foreword

Love, like life, is a journey filled with unexpected turns—sometimes joyful, sometimes heartbreaking. This book was born from a place of love & drafted during vulnerability, where dreams collided with reality, and emotions ran deep. It captures the complexity of love, not just in its bright, passionate moments, but also in the quiet struggles, painful stories and lovable endings.

As I wrote, I found myself reflecting on the fragility of human connections, the weight of misunderstandings, and the silience that love demands of us. The characters, though fictional, carry pieces of my experiences and lessons—of love lost, found, and everything in between.

For anyone who has ever loved deeply, hurt silently, or healed slowly, this story is for you. I hope it speaks to your heart as much as it has to mine.

"*With gratitude and hope,*
-Mihir Bommisetty"

Preface

Every story is born from a seed—an idea, a moment, or a feeling that grows and takes root in the soul. This particular story began as a reflection of my own journey through love, loss, and self-discovery. What started as a personal experience has evolved into the lives of Priya, Aarav, and Rishi, characters who navigate the deep web of emotions, choices, and consequences that love weaves around us.

Writing this novel has been a chaotic experience during the rough phase i've been through. It allowed me to delve into the beauty and the pain that come with love—the moments of euphoria when everything seems perfect, and the darker days when misunderstandings, insecurities, and silence create a chaos too wide to cross. The story mirrors the complexities of relationships i face, we all face, the longing for connection, and the struggle to hold onto something fragile yet powerful. The beauty of togetherness that replnish the love what everyone wish for.

At its heart, this book is a testament to the resilience of the human spirit, resonance of emotions, the ways we confront love and heartache. Hardships we all go through to work on the misunderstandings. It is about finding ourselves, even in the midst of losing something precious. Through these pages, I hope you find yourselves, your loved ones, pieces of your own journey, your own reflections, tonnes of sadness, and perhaps a little bit of comfort.

Thank you for joining me on this emotional journey. May you find as much in these pages as I did in writing them. I surely assure you that this piece of art i chose to explain the beauty of relationship is always to find the one who always comfort in this life called life lessons.

Acknowledgements

Writing a novel is not just an individual interest. It's the culmination of many moments, people, and experiences that have come together, making this creative process possible. As I sit down to reflect on this journey as a author, I realize how fortunate I am to have had the unwavering support, encouragement, and love of many wonderful individuals. This book is as much theirs as it is mine.

First and foremost, to my family: there are no words that can truly value the depth of my gratitude. To my parents, who have been the rock support of my life, you have been the ones who believed in me when I didn't believe in myself. Through every high and low, every late night of thoughts, and every draft that seemed never-ending, you provided me with the comfort and reassurance I needed to keep going. Your love has been the light that guided me through some of the darkest moments of this creative journey. This book would not have come out this good without your strength and belief in me.

To my friends, thank you for your patience and understanding when i was in writers block and be blank for days. You all never failed to be there, cheering me on from the sidelines. In particular.

I also want to express my deepest thanks to the early readers who patiently offered their time and insights. You were one of the first to see this story in its raw, unfinished form, and your enthusiasm for the characters and plot helped give me the confidence to keep moving forward. Your thoughtful questions, and encouragement pushed me to take the manuscript to better versions, and I am forever thankful to you.

To the artists, authors, and creators whose work has inspired me along the way, thank you for reminding me of the power of storytelling.

Lastly, to every reader who picks up this book: thank you. You are the reason stories like this one exist. Writing is an intimate act of vulnerability, and sharing this story with you is both exciting and humbling. My deepest hope is that these pages resonate with you, that you find pieces of yourself in the characters, and that the story stays with you long after you've finished reading. Thank you for allowing me to share this journey with you.

As I reflect on the completion of this book, I feel an overwhelming sense of gratitude. From the very first word to the final edit, this process has been one of discovery, of learning, and of growth—not just as a writer, but as a person. This book is a testament to the love and support that surrounded me throughout its creation, and for that, I am extremly thankful.

Thank you, all, from the bottom of my heart.

"With love and gratitude,
-Mihir Bommisetty"

Prologue

Priya sat by the window, holding a cup of tea that had gone cold. Outside, the world kept moving—cars passing, people talking—but inside, everything felt still. It had been weeks since she had last seen Aarav, but she couldn't stop thinking about him. His memory filled every corner of her mind. She can't process any words to draft the story she's working on from months although the deadlines are near.

Their relationship used to be full of laughter, dreams, and promises. But now, there was only silence. Priya had always believed love could survive anything, but she was starting to understand how fragile love really was. Sometimes, one small mistake was enough to break it apart. As she looked out the window, she wondered how everything had gone so wrong.

Across the city, Aarav sat in his studio, surrounded by photographs. His camera had always helped him make sense of the world, capturing small moments of beauty. But lately, even photography didn't feel the same. Every picture reminded him of Priya and the future they had dreamed of. That dream now felt out of reach.

Priya has to met her ex which drives this relationship crazy. As they're ex-es their conversations were easy. They once shared the love for each other and has some best moments in life. But deep down, Priya knew something was missing. A part of her still wants Aarav.

They had loved each other deeply, but now they stood at a point where they had to make a choice; whether to hold on to their past or let it go and start new lives.

As the sun set, Priya closed her eyes and took a deep breath. She didn't know what the future would bring, but she knew that nothing would ever be the same again. The story of Priya, Aarav, and Rishi was just beginning, but the choices they made would change their lives forever.

1

Chai Aur Kahani - The Beginning of Us

The café was small, tucked into a quiet corner of the bustling city of Mumbai. Outside, the sound of honking cars and chattering crowds created a chaotic symphony. But inside, it was peaceful. The walls were lined with bookshelves that housed old paperbacks, their spines worn from being read and re-read. The air was rich with the scent of freshly brewed chai, mingled with the faint aroma of cinnamon and cardamom.

Priya sat at a small table near the window, her fingers wrapped around a warm cup of chai. She was lost in thought, staring out at the busy street but not really seeing it. The pages of her notebook lay open in front of her, but no words filled them. The writer's block had crept in weeks ago, and no matter how much she tried, her mind felt like an empty well, dry and barren.

She sighed and took a sip of her chai. It was comforting, the warmth spreading through her, but it didn't ease the frustration gnawing at her. She was supposed to be working on the next chapter of her novel, a novel that her publisher was eagerly waiting for. But here she was, staring at blank pages once again.

The sound of a camera shutter clicking broke through her thoughts. Priya looked up, her eyes catching the source of the noise. A man was standing near the entrance, his camera aimed at the window where sunlight streamed in, casting soft shadows on the floor. His focus was intense, completely absorbed in the moment, as if he saw something in the ordinary scene that no one else could.

He was tall, with tousled black hair that looked like it hadn't seen a comb in days. His jeans were worn and faded, and his shirt was rumpled, the kind of casual appearance that suggested he was more concerned with capturing the world through his lens than with how he looked. There was something about him, something that made Priya curious.

Before she could look away, he lowered the camera and caught her gaze. For a moment, they simply stared at each other, neither moving nor speaking. Then, he smiled, a small, almost shy smile and raised his camera, gesturing as if to ask for permission to take her photo.

Priya blinked in surprise. No one had ever asked to photograph her before, and she wasn't sure how to respond. But there was something about the way he looked at her, as if he saw something worth capturing. Slowly, she nodded.

He raised the camera again, his finger hovering over the shutter button. Priya suddenly felt self-conscious, unsure of how to pose or where to look. But he didn't seem to care about perfection. He clicked the shutter, once, twice, and then lowered the camera, looking at the small screen with a satisfied expression.

"Thank you," he said, his voice deep but soft, as he walked over to her table.

Priya smiled awkwardly, unsure of what to say. "Do I get to see the picture?"

He chuckled, holding out the camera so she could see. The photo was simple, just her sitting at the table, her fingers still wrapped around the cup of chai, her eyes staring out the window. But there was something beautiful about it, something quiet and introspective that she hadn't seen in herself before.

"It's beautiful," she said, surprised by how much she liked it.

"It's easy when the subject is interesting," he replied, his tone light but sincere. "I'm Aarav, by the way."

"Priya," she said, offering her hand. He shook it, his grip warm and firm.

"You're a writer?" Aarav asked, nodding towards the open notebook on the table.

"I try to be," Priya said with a small laugh. "But right now, I'm just staring at blank pages and hoping inspiration strikes."

"Writer's block?"

She nodded. "Yeah. It's like my brain has decided to go on vacation without me."

Aarav smiled, sitting down across from her. "I know the feeling. Sometimes, when I'm out with my camera, it's like I see the world, but I can't capture it the way I want to. The pictures just... don't work."

Priya tilted her head, intrigued. "But you seem like you're good at it. The photo you took just now—it was perfect."

"It's all about the moment," Aarav said, his gaze flicking out the window for a second. "Sometimes, you just have to let go of the pressure and let the moment guide you. Maybe it's the same with writing?"

Priya thought about that. She had been putting so much pressure on herself lately, worrying about deadlines, expectations, and whether her next book would live up to the last one. Maybe Aarav was right. Maybe she needed to stop thinking so hard and just... write.

"You might be onto something," she admitted with a smile. "I'll give it a try."

They talked for a while longer, about photography, writing, and the way art seemed to be an endless pursuit of something just out of reach. Priya found herself opening up to him in a way she hadn't with anyone else. There was something about Aarav that made her feel comfortable, like they had known each other for longer than just an hour.

When the café started to empty out and the sun dipped low in the sky, Aarav stood up, slinging his camera bag over his shoulder.

"I should get going," he said. "But it was nice meeting you, Priya. I hope you find your inspiration soon."

"Thanks, Aarav," she said, standing up as well. "And thanks for the picture."

He smiled again, that same shy smile that had caught her attention earlier. "Anytime."

As he walked out the door, Priya sat back down, looking at the blank page in front of her. But this time, it didn't feel so daunting. She picked up her pen, letting the words flow without overthinking them.

The beginning of a new chapter, both in her notebook and, perhaps, in her life.

2

Silent Connection

The next few days passed in a blur of words and chai. Priya found herself returning to the same café, her notebook filling up with scribbled ideas, fragments of dialogue, and potential scenes for her novel. Aarav's advice had worked. She had let go of the pressure to be perfect, and in doing so, her writing had finally started to flow again. It wasn't perfect, far from it but it was progress.

Still, despite the creative surge, something else lingered in her mind: Aarav. She hadn't expected him to leave such an impression after just one meeting. There was a quiet charm about him, an energy that made her curious. She found herself thinking about him at odd moments, wondering where he was, what he was photographing, and whether he ever thought about their conversation.

She tried to push the thoughts away. After all, she didn't know him beyond that single hour in the café. And besides, she had bigger things to worry about like finishing her novel before her deadline.

One evening, as she sat at the café, her pen scratching against the paper, her phone buzzed on the table. She glanced at the screen and saw a message from her best friend, Rhea.

Rhea: Hey, how's the writing going? Haven't heard from you in days!

Priya smiled and quickly typed a response.

Priya: Finally making progress. You'd be proud of me!

Rhea: I'm ALWAYS proud of you. We need to catch up soon. I miss our chai sessions!

Priya: How about tomorrow? Same café?

Rhea: Done. Can't wait!

Priya put her phone down, feeling a little lighter. Rhea had been her best friend since college, and their weekly chai sessions were one of the few constants in her life. It would be nice to take a break from writing and catch up.

The next afternoon, Priya arrived at the café a little early. She ordered her usual cup of chai and found a table by the window. As she waited, she let her eyes wander, watching the steady stream of people walking by outside. It was a warm day, and the city felt alive with energy.

She was so lost in thought that she didn't notice Rhea slide into the seat across from her until she heard her voice.

"So, this is where all the magic happens?" Rhea teased, gesturing to Priya's open notebook.

Priya laughed. "More like where I stare at blank pages for hours."

Rhea shook her head, her long earrings swaying as she did. "You're too hard on yourself. You always get there in the end."

"Maybe. But it's taking longer this time."

"Which is fine," Rhea said, her voice gentle but firm. "You can't rush the creative process. And honestly, you need to give yourself more credit. You've written two bestsellers! You're amazing, Priya."

Priya smiled, appreciating Rhea's unwavering support. "Thanks. I guess I just... I don't know, I feel like something's missing. Like I'm not inspired the way I used to be."

Rhea raised an eyebrow. "Something or someone?"

Priya rolled her eyes. "Please, not this again."

But Rhea wasn't letting it go. "I'm serious. When was the last time you went out and met someone? You're always buried in your writing. You need a break. Meet someone new. Fall in love."

"I don't have time for that," Priya protested, though a small part of her wondered if Rhea had a point.

"You don't have time, or you're too scared?" Rhea asked, her tone gentle but probing.

Priya looked down at her chai, avoiding the question. It wasn't that she hadn't thought about it—about love, about relationships. But her past had taught her to be cautious. After her last relationship ended badly, she had thrown herself into her work, convincing herself that writing was enough.

Rhea sighed, reaching across the table to touch Priya's hand. "You deserve to be happy, Priya. And you deserve someone who makes you feel like you're the only person in the world."

Priya swallowed, feeling a lump form in her throat. "Maybe. But I haven't found that person yet."

"Well, maybe you just need to keep your eyes open," Rhea said with a wink.

Priya laughed, grateful for Rhea's lightheartedness. They spent the rest of the afternoon catching up, talking about everything from Rhea's work to their favorite movies. For a while, Priya forgot about her novel, about her doubts, and even about Aarav.

But later that night, as she lay in bed, staring at the ceiling, her mind drifted back to him. She wondered if their paths would cross again. And if they did, what would happen?

The next day, Priya found herself back at the café, her notebook open in front of her. But today, the words weren't flowing as easily. She stared at the page, tapping her pen against the table, feeling the familiar frustration creeping back in.

She was about to give up and pack her things when she heard a voice.

"Still working on that novel?"

She looked up and saw Aarav standing there, his camera slung over his shoulder, his familiar smile tugging at the corners of his mouth.

Priya felt her heart skip a beat. "You again," she said, unable to hide her smile.

"Guilty," Aarav said, sliding into the chair across from her. "Mind if I join you?"

"Not at all," Priya said, closing her notebook. "But I should warn you, I haven't made much progress since we last talked."

Aarav raised an eyebrow. "Really? I thought you were on a roll."

"I was. But now I'm stuck again," Priya admitted with a sigh.

Aarav nodded, his gaze thoughtful. "Sometimes, when I hit a creative block, I like to change my perspective. Try looking at things from a different angle."

"Different angle?" Priya asked, intrigued.

"Yeah. Like, instead of sitting here staring at the page, maybe you need to get out. Experience something new. Find inspiration in the world around you."

Priya smiled, remembering what Rhea had said about meeting someone new and experiencing life outside of her writing. "You sound like my best friend."

"She sounds like a smart person," Aarav said with a grin. "So, what do you say? Want to go for a walk?"

Priya hesitated for a moment. She had been so focused on her writing, on meeting her deadline, that she hadn't even considered taking a break. But maybe Aarav was right. Maybe she needed to step away from the page for a while.

"Sure," she said, standing up and grabbing her bag. "A walk sounds nice."

They left the café together, stepping out into the warm afternoon sun. As they walked, Aarav pointed out little details that Priya would have never noticed on her own—a street vendor arranging flowers, the way the light reflected off a puddle, the quiet hum of the city in the background.

For the first time in a long time, Priya felt like she was seeing the world in a new way, through Aarav's eyes. And as they walked side by side, she realized that maybe, just maybe, Rhea had been right. Maybe it was time to let someone new into her life.

But as they rounded a corner and Aarav snapped a photo of a passing rickshaw, Priya felt a flicker of uncertainty. She had been hurt before. Could she really open herself up again?

3

Dreams We Shared

The sun was setting, casting a golden hue over the city streets as Priya and Aarav walked in silence. For Priya, the quiet between them wasn't awkward. It was peaceful. She found herself stealing glances at Aarav as he snapped pictures of seemingly mundane objects—the side of an old building, a bicycle leaning against a lamppost, the reflection of the sky in a puddle. Each click of his camera made her curious about what he saw through his lens.

"You have a way of seeing things," Priya said finally, breaking the silence.

Aarav looked at her and smiled. "It's the little things that make the big picture."

His words hung in the air, and Priya felt an unexpected warmth spread through her. She had always been the kind of person who focused on the larger story, the grand moments, but here was someone who paid attention to the details. She liked that about him—how he could find beauty in the smallest of things.

As they continued walking, they passed a group of children playing cricket in a narrow alley. Aarav paused, watching them with a soft smile on his face. He raised his camera, capturing the moment.

"Do you ever wonder what happens to the people you photograph?" Priya asked, stopping beside him.

Aarav lowered his camera and turned to her, his expression thoughtful. "Sometimes. But I like to think that I'm capturing a piece of their story, even if I don't know how it ends."

Priya nodded, understanding the sentiment. In many ways, her writing was similar. She created characters, gave them life, but once the story ended, they were out of her hands. They belonged to the readers, to the world.

"I think that's why I love photography," Aarav continued. "It's like freezing a moment in time, but there's always more to the story than what's in the frame."

Priya smiled. "You're more philosophical than I expected."

He laughed. "I get that a lot."

They walked a bit further, the sun dipping lower on the horizon. Priya found herself wondering more about Aarav's story. What had brought him to this city? What was it that had sparked his passion for photography? She wanted to ask, but she wasn't sure if she should. After all, they were practically strangers.

But just as she was about to ask, Aarav spoke first. "So, what's your novel about?"

Priya hesitated, unsure of how to describe it. "It's... complicated," she said finally. "It's about a woman who's trying to find herself. She's lost in a lot of ways, and she's trying to figure out what she really wants in life."

Aarav raised an eyebrow. "Sounds like someone I know."

Priya laughed softly. "Maybe. It's hard to write something that doesn't come from personal experience, I guess."

He nodded. "I get that. My best photos are the ones that mean something to me. It's easier to capture something when you've lived it."

Priya looked at him, surprised by how easily he understood. There was something about Aarav that made her feel like she didn't have to explain herself. He just... got it.

They continued walking until they reached a park, where Aarav led them to a bench. They sat in comfortable silence for a while, watching the world go by.

After a few minutes, Aarav turned to her. "You know, I've been thinking about your writing process. Maybe you're stuck because you're trying too hard to figure everything out. Sometimes, it's okay to not have all the answers. Just write what feels right."

Priya considered his words, realizing that he might be onto something. She had been so focused on getting everything perfect, on making sure her story made sense, that she had forgotten to let herself explore.

"Maybe you're right," she said, her voice soft.

"I'm always right," Aarav said with a grin.

Priya laughed, shaking her head. "I'll remember that."

As the sun finally dipped below the horizon, casting long shadows across the park, Priya felt something shift inside her. Maybe it was Aarav's words, or maybe it was just the simple act of stepping away from her desk and seeing the world in a new light, but for the first time in weeks, she felt a sense of clarity.

She didn't have all the answers. But maybe, just maybe, she didn't need them right now.

4

Wanderers in Love

The following week passed in a blur of writing sessions and late-night texts exchanged between Priya and Aarav. He had quickly become a part of her daily routine—an unexpected but welcome distraction. Their conversations ranged from light-hearted banter to deep discussions about life, creativity, and everything in between.

Priya found herself looking forward to their talks. Aarav had a way of making her feel seen, understood in a way that she hadn't experienced in a long time. It scared her, but it also excited her.

One evening, as they sat at their usual table in the café, Aarav brought up a photography project he was working on.

"I've been thinking about doing a series on the city," he said, tapping his fingers on the table. "But I want to capture it from a different perspective."

Priya raised an eyebrow. "What do you mean?"

"I want to show the city through the eyes of different people. Like, what does the city look like to someone who's just moved here? Or to someone who's lived here their whole life? Everyone sees it differently."

Priya nodded, intrigued. "That's a great idea. Have you started shooting yet?"

"Not yet. I'm still figuring out who I want to focus on. But I think I know where to start."

Priya leaned forward, curious. "Where?"

Aarav met her gaze, his eyes twinkling. "You."

She blinked, taken aback. "Me?"

"Yeah. You're new to the city, right? I want to see it through your eyes."

Priya hesitated. The idea of being photographed made her uncomfortable, but there was something about the way Aarav asked that made it hard to say no.

"I don't know," she said slowly. "I'm not really photogenic."

Aarav laughed. "That's not true. Besides, it's not about being photogenic. It's about capturing your perspective."

Priya bit her lip, considering his words. She had never been the type to enjoy being in front of the camera, but this felt different. This was about storytelling, about seeing the world through her eyes.

"Okay," she said finally. "I'll do it."

Aarav grinned. "Great. We'll start tomorrow."

The next day, they met in the early morning, just as the sun was rising. The city was quiet, the streets still waking up. Aarav led her to different spots around the city—places she had passed a hundred times but had never really noticed.

As he snapped photos, he asked her questions about her experience in the city. What had surprised her? What had disappointed her? What had made her fall in love with it?

Priya answered honestly, and as she spoke, she realized that her feelings about the city mirrored her feelings about life. It was messy, unpredictable, and sometimes overwhelming. But it was also beautiful, full of moments that took her breath away.

When Aarav finished, they sat on a bench, reviewing the photos on his camera.

"These are amazing," Priya said, her voice filled with awe.

Aarav smiled. "They're your story."

As they sat there, side by side, Priya felt a connection growing between them—something deeper than friendship, something she wasn't sure how to define yet.

But as she looked at the photos of herself, captured through Aarav's lens, she realized that maybe, just maybe, she was ready to take the next step. Not just in her writing, but in her life.

5

Fragile Bonds

Priya stared at the blinking cursor on her screen. She had written, deleted, and rewritten the same paragraph at least five times, but nothing felt right. Her mind kept drifting back to her day with Aarav. The way he had captured the city through her eyes, and the way he had, in turn, captured something deeper about her. She hadn't expected to feel so seen, so understood.

With a sigh, she closed her laptop and stood up, stretching her arms above her head. Her phone buzzed on the table, and she reached for it, half-expecting another message from Aarav. But instead, it was her editor.

Deadline is approaching. Any chance we'll see some pages soon? the text read.

Priya's heart sank. She knew she was behind, but the pressure only seemed to make the words harder to find. She sat back down, determined to write something—anything—but before she could start, there was a knock at the door.

Frowning, she opened it to find Aarav standing there, holding a coffee cup in each hand and a mischievous grin on his face.

"I brought fuel," he said, handing her one of the cups. "Thought you might need it."

Priya took the cup, smiling despite herself. "How did you know?"

"I've been there," Aarav said with a shrug. "Creative block is a real thing."

She stepped aside to let him in, and they settled onto the couch. Priya sipped her coffee, feeling the warmth spread through her, and for the first time that day, a sense of calm settled over her.

"So," Aarav said after a moment, "how's the writing going?"

Priya made a face. "Terribly. I can't seem to get anything right."

Aarav frowned. "What's wrong?"

"I don't know," Priya admitted. "I feel like I'm stuck. Like I'm trying too hard to make the story perfect, and it's just not coming out the way I want."

Aarav was silent for a moment, as if considering her words. Then, he set his cup down and leaned forward. "You know what I think?"

Priya raised an eyebrow. "What?"

"I think you're overthinking it. Sometimes, the best stories are the ones that come naturally. You can always go back and edit later, but right now, you just need to get the words out."

Priya sighed, knowing he was right but still feeling the weight of the deadline looming over her. "It's easier said than done."

"Of course it is," Aarav said with a smile. "But you've got this. You're an amazing writer, Priya. You just need to trust yourself."

His words sent a warmth through her, and she felt a flicker of inspiration spark inside her. Maybe he was right. Maybe she was too focused on the end result and needed to just let the story flow.

"Okay," she said finally. "I'll try."

Aarav grinned. "That's the spirit."

They sat in comfortable silence for a while, sipping their coffee, and Priya felt the tension in her shoulders begin to ease. She glanced over at Aarav, wondering if he knew just how much his presence had helped her. In the few weeks they had known each other, he had become a constant source of encouragement and support. She wasn't sure how it had happened, but somehow, he had become an important part of her life.

And that scared her.

She had been through enough heartbreak to know how fragile relationships could be. But with Aarav, things felt different. There was an ease between them, a connection that went beyond words. It was as if they were two pieces of a puzzle that had just clicked into place.

But even so, Priya couldn't help but wonder if it was too good to be true. Could she really let herself fall for him? Or was she setting herself up for more heartache?

Shaking the thoughts from her mind, Priya turned her attention back to her laptop. She opened the document, staring at the blank page. But this time, instead of feeling overwhelmed, she felt a sense of calm. She could do this. She just needed to trust herself.

Taking a deep breath, she began to type.

6

Whispers of Doubt

Days turned into weeks, and Priya found herself falling into a comfortable rhythm with Aarav. They spent more time together, exploring the city, sharing stories, and laughing at each other's jokes. It was easy, natural, and for the first time in a long while, Priya felt truly happy.

Her writing had also taken a turn for the better. With Aarav's encouragement, she stopped worrying about perfection and started letting the words flow. Her novel was finally taking shape, and with each page she wrote, she felt more confident in her ability to tell the story she had been struggling with for so long.

But just as things seemed to be falling into place, a piece of Priya's past resurfaced in the most unexpected way.

One afternoon, as Priya sat in the café waiting for Aarav, her phone buzzed with a notification. She glanced at the screen, expecting a message from him, but instead, it was an email.

From Rishi.

Priya's heart skipped a beat. Rishi was her ex—the one who had broken her heart and left her questioning everything about herself. She hadn't spoken to him in over a year, and seeing his name in her inbox sent a wave of emotions crashing over her.

With trembling fingers, she opened the email.

Hey Priya,

I know it's been a while, but I've been thinking about you a lot lately. I miss you. I've been doing a lot of soul-searching, and I realize now that I made a mistake. I shouldn't have let you go.

I don't know if you'll even read this, but I just wanted to reach out. Maybe we could meet up and talk? I'd love to see you again.

Rishi

Priya stared at the screen, her mind racing. She hadn't expected this. Not now, not when things were finally starting to feel right in her life.

Her thoughts were interrupted by the sound of the café door opening, and she looked up to see Aarav walking in, his usual smile in place. But as he approached, Priya quickly closed her laptop, her heart pounding in her chest.

"Hey," Aarav said, sitting down across from her. "You okay?"

Priya forced a smile. "Yeah, I'm fine. Just... got some work stuff on my mind."

Aarav raised an eyebrow, clearly sensing that something was off, but he didn't push. "Okay, well, if you ever need to talk, I'm here."

Priya nodded, grateful for his understanding, but her mind was still on the email. What was she supposed to do now? Should she respond? Should she meet with Rishi? Or should she just delete the email and pretend it never happened?

As she sat there, staring at Aarav, the weight of her past and the uncertainty of her future pressed down on her. She had thought she had moved on, but now she wasn't so sure.

And in that moment, Priya realized that the choices she made in the coming days could change everything.

7

Breaking Point

Priya spent the next few days wrestling with the email from Rishi. She couldn't shake the memories of their relationship—both the good times and the heartbreak that had followed. It was difficult to reconcile the person she had been with Rishi and the woman she was now, someone who had begun to find her footing again, especially with Aarav by her side.

During a late-night writing session, Priya finally decided to respond. Her fingers hovered over the keyboard, hesitating. After drafting and deleting several versions, she settled on a simple reply.

Hi Rishi,

It's good to hear from you. I'm surprised, but I hope you're doing well. Let's talk sometime.

Priya

With her heart racing, she hit send. There. It was done. A part of her felt relieved; another part felt anxious about where this could lead.

The next day, Aarav noticed she was quieter than usual during their coffee date. "What's going on in that brilliant mind of yours?" he asked, tilting his head slightly as they sat across from each other.

Priya forced a smile, pushing her cup away. "Just... thinking about some things."

Aarav studied her for a moment, concern etching his features. "You know you can tell me anything, right?"

She wanted to tell him everything, but the weight of her past felt too heavy to share. Instead, she nodded, feeling a pang of guilt for not being completely open with him.

"Okay," Aarav said, still watching her closely. "But I'm here whenever you need to talk."

"Thanks," she replied softly. The warmth of his words made her heart swell, but she couldn't shake the dread that filled her with each moment that passed. How could she be moving forward with Aarav while still dealing with Rishi?

Days passed, and Priya found herself slipping into a routine of avoidance. She spent more time writing and less time reflecting on her feelings. The manuscript was coming along beautifully, thanks in no small part to Aarav's support, but the unresolved situation with Rishi loomed over her like a dark cloud.

Then, one rainy evening, her phone buzzed with a message from Rishi.

Can we meet tomorrow? I really want to talk.

Priya's heart raced as she stared at the screen. A million thoughts swirled in her mind. She felt the tug of nostalgia, the thrill of old feelings, but also the warmth of her growing bond with Aarav.

What would she say? How would it affect her relationship with Aarav? In a moment of clarity, she decided to be honest with Aarav about her meeting.

"Hey, can we talk?" Priya asked, her voice barely above a whisper as she and Aarav walked through the park later that week.

“Of course,” Aarav replied, concern flickering across his face. They found a bench, and she took a deep breath.

“I got an email from Rishi,” she admitted, her heart pounding. “He wants to meet.”

Aarav’s expression shifted, and for a moment, he looked hurt. “And what do you want?”

“I don’t know,” Priya admitted, her voice trembling. “I thought I had moved on, but this is all so confusing. I just—”

“You need to figure out what you want, Priya,” Aarav interrupted gently. “But just remember, I’m here for you, no matter what.”

She nodded, feeling a swell of gratitude for his understanding. “Thank you. I promise I’ll be honest with you.”

As they walked home, Priya felt the weight of her decision hanging heavy in the air. Meeting Rishi could bring closure—or it could open old wounds.

8

A World Apart

The next day, Priya found herself standing outside a quaint little café where she and Rishi had shared countless memories. The familiarity of the place made her heart race, memories flooding back as she pushed open the door.

Rishi was already seated at a table in the corner, his back to her. As she approached, he turned around, a nervous smile spreading across his face. The sight of him stirred a mixture of emotions within her.

"Hey," he said, his voice warm but cautious.

"Hi," Priya replied, sliding into the seat across from him. The air between them felt thick with unspoken words.

"I'm glad you came," Rishi said, looking into her eyes as if searching for something. "I wasn't sure if you would."

Priya forced a smile. "I wasn't sure either."

For a moment, they both sat in silence, the clinking of cups and quiet chatter surrounding them. Priya felt the weight of their history pressing down, urging her to break the silence.

"I got your email," she said finally. "You mentioned you wanted to talk?"

Rishi nodded, his gaze dropping to the table. “Yeah, I’ve been doing a lot of thinking. I’ve missed you, Priya. I made a mistake letting you go.”

Priya felt a pang in her chest, but she steeled herself. “You hurt me, Rishi. It took me a long time to move on.”

“I know,” he said, his voice thick with regret. “I’ve spent the last year trying to figure out what I want. I’ve realized how important you are to me.”

“Why now?” Priya asked, frustration creeping into her voice. “Why did it take you so long to realize that?”

Rishi looked pained, his expression softening. “Because I was scared, Priya. Scared of commitment, scared of being vulnerable. But I’ve changed. I want to make things right.”

Priya stared at him, torn between the comfort of their past and the uncertainty of the present. “And what does that mean? Are you asking for another chance?”

Rishi reached across the table, his hand inches from hers. “I’m asking for a chance to explain, to show you that I’ve grown. I know I messed up, but I want to try again.”

Priya pulled her hand back, her heart racing. “And what about the pain you caused? The doubt you planted in my mind?”

“I can’t change the past,” Rishi said, desperation creeping into his voice. “But I can show you that I’m different now. I just need you to give me that opportunity.”

Priya felt her resolve waver. Memories of their love, their laughter, and the dreams they had shared flooded her mind. But she also remembered the heartbreak, the feeling of betrayal. The scars he had left behind were still fresh in her memory.

“Rishi, I don’t know if I can just forget what happened,” she said softly. “It’s not that simple.”

He looked defeated, running a hand through his hair. "I get it. I really do. But I wouldn't be here if I didn't think it was worth it."

For the first time in a long time, Priya felt the weight of her emotions crashing over her. She had built a new life, a new connection with Aarav. But here was Rishi, offering her a glimpse into their past—a past that had once been beautiful but had ultimately shattered.

"I need time to think," Priya said, her voice barely above a whisper.

Rishi nodded, his expression a mix of understanding and disappointment. "Take all the time you need. I'll be here."

As she left the café, Priya felt a swirl of emotions, a tug-of-war between the past and the present. She had a choice to make—one that could alter the course of her life forever.

9

Echos of Goodbye

Priya spent the next few days in a daze, her mind constantly replaying her meeting with Rishi. Each time she thought about him, the memories flooded back—both the happy and the painful. Despite her better judgment, she found herself comparing Rishi's return with the warmth she felt when she was with Aarav.

Aarav noticed her distraction, and one evening while they were sitting in his cozy apartment, he asked, "What's on your mind, Priya?"

"Just... life," she replied, trying to sound casual as she fiddled with her coffee mug.

"You've been distant lately," Aarav pressed, his eyes searching hers. "I don't want to push you, but if something's bothering you, I'm here."

Priya hesitated, contemplating whether to share her struggles. "It's just work and some personal stuff," she finally said, opting for vague honesty.

He nodded, though she could tell he sensed there was more. "You know I care about you, right? Whatever it is, you can tell me."

A surge of warmth enveloped her at his words. She appreciated his concern, but how could she explain the mess that was her heart? Rishi's sudden reappearance complicated everything she had begun to build with Aarav.

"Thank you," she said, forcing a smile. "I appreciate it. I really do."

That evening, Priya tried to focus on her writing, but the words felt stagnant. Her fingers hovered over the keyboard, but her mind was elsewhere. She wondered if she was making the right decision by keeping her past with Rishi a secret from Aarav. She wanted to be honest, but the thought of hurting him was unbearable.

Days turned into weeks, and her internal struggle deepened. Every time she met Aarav, they shared laughs and warmth, but the shadow of Rishi loomed over her, gnawing at her resolve.

One day, as she sat in her favorite café, sipping a chai latte, her phone buzzed with a text from Rishi.

Can we talk again?

The simplicity of his message made her heart race. She glanced around, half-expecting Aarav to appear at any moment. She was torn—was she ready to reopen that chapter of her life?

After a moment of hesitation, she replied.

Sure. When?

How about tomorrow?

She stared at the message, knowing that seeing Rishi again could either bring closure or reignite old flames. In the pit of her stomach, she felt a mix of excitement and dread.

The next day, she met Rishi at the same café where they had previously talked. As she walked in, she spotted him at a corner table, his expression serious.

"Hey," she greeted, forcing a smile as she sat down.

"Hi," Rishi replied, his voice low. "Thanks for coming."

"Of course," she said, feeling the tension in the air. "What did you want to discuss?"

"I've been thinking a lot about us. I know I hurt you, and I'm truly sorry for that," Rishi began, his eyes earnest. "But I've also realized how much I still care about you. I'm ready to be the person you need me to be."

Priya felt her heart race, the weight of his words pressing down on her. "Rishi, I don't know if we can just pick up where we left off. Things have changed."

"I understand that," he said quickly. "But I believe we can work through it. I've done a lot of soul-searching, and I know I can be better for you."

Priya's mind raced. Here was Rishi, offering her a chance to revisit their past. But was it worth the risk?

"Look, I appreciate you wanting to make things right, but I'm not the same person I was back then," Priya said, her voice steady. "I've started to build a life without you. There's someone else now."

Rishi's expression fell, but he quickly masked it with a determined look. "Aarav, right?"

"Yes," she replied, feeling a pang of guilt. "He's been there for me. He's kind and supportive."

"Then why are you here with me?" Rishi challenged gently.

"Because I need to confront my past," Priya admitted, her voice breaking slightly. "But I also need to be honest about my feelings. I don't want to hurt Aarav."

Rishi looked contemplative, nodding slowly. "I can respect that. But you should also consider what you truly want. It's okay to take your time to figure things out."

Priya felt a flicker of hope, yet uncertainty hung in the air. She knew she had to tread carefully; her heart was fragile, and she didn't want to lose what she had with Aarav.

"Thank you for understanding," she said softly. "I just need some time."

10

Lost Without You

As she left the café, Priya felt a sense of relief wash over her. Meeting Rishi had given her some closure, but it had also opened a floodgate of emotions she hadn't expected.

She needed to talk to Aarav. As she walked through the park, her thoughts spun with everything that had happened. She found herself wishing that things could be simpler—wishing she could just focus on her relationship with Aarav without the ghosts of her past haunting her.

Later that evening, Priya invited Aarav over for dinner. As she cooked, she felt nervous energy coursing through her. Would he understand? Would he be angry?

When Aarav arrived, he brought flowers and a smile that lit up her dimly lit apartment. "These are for you," he said, handing her the blooms.

"They're beautiful! Thank you," she replied, feeling warmth spread in her chest. They settled down for dinner, laughter filling the room as they shared stories from their day. Yet, despite the lightness of the moment, Priya felt the heaviness of what she needed to confess.

After dinner, as they sipped wine, Priya decided to broach the topic. "Aarav, can we talk about something important?"

He looked up, concern flashing in his eyes. "Of course. What's on your mind?"

Taking a deep breath, she began, "I met Rishi again."

Aarav's expression shifted; his gaze focused intently on her. "What happened?"

"He... he wants to make amends. He said he's realized how much he cares about me," Priya explained, her voice trembling slightly. "But I also told him that I'm not the same person I was back then. I'm with you now, and I want to be with you."

Aarav's silence hung in the air, thick with tension. Finally, he spoke, his voice steady but laced with emotion. "And how do you feel about that?"

"I don't know, Aarav. Part of me feels drawn to him, but another part of me knows I want to be with you. You've been my rock," Priya confessed, her heart racing.

"I appreciate your honesty," Aarav said, his expression unreadable. "But it's tough to hear. You're still processing your feelings for him, and that's okay. Just know that I care about you deeply."

"I don't want to hurt you," Priya said, her voice breaking. "I need time to figure this out, and I hope you can be patient with me."

Aarav sighed, his shoulders slumping slightly. "I don't want to pressure you, but I also don't want to be in a relationship where you're not fully invested. You deserve to figure this out, and I deserve to know where I stand."

Tears welled in Priya's eyes, the weight of the situation feeling unbearable. "I know, and I'm so sorry. I just wish things were easier."

Aarav reached across the table, taking her hand in his. "We'll get through this. Just know that I'm here for you, no matter what."

In that moment, Priya felt both relief and despair. She had opened the door to honesty, yet the uncertainty remained. As she gazed into Aarav's eyes, she felt the tug-of-war in her heart intensify.

She had to choose.

11

Fading Memories

In the days that followed her conversation with Aarav, Priya felt as if she were walking a tightrope. She wanted to explore her feelings for Rishi but was terrified of losing Aarav in the process. Every time she met with Aarav, she cherished the connection they shared, yet the specter of her past loomed ever larger.

One evening, as she sat alone in her apartment, Priya received a text from Rishi, asking if they could meet again. She stared at the screen, her heart racing. She knew that this meeting could either be the closure she needed or the beginning of a confusing new chapter in her life.

After a moment of contemplation, she replied.

Sure. Let's meet tomorrow.

The next day, they met at a quaint little park, surrounded by blooming flowers and soft chirping birds. The beauty of the setting contrasted sharply with the turmoil inside Priya. As she approached, she saw Rishi sitting on a bench, his expression thoughtful.

"Hey," he said, standing up as she arrived.

"Hey," she replied, her heart pounding. "What did you want to talk about?"

"I wanted to apologize again," he started, his tone earnest. "I know I messed things up, and I've spent a lot of time thinking about us. I can't shake the feeling that we might still have something."

Priya felt a flicker of warmth at his words, but she quickly pushed it away. "Rishi, I'm not here to reopen old wounds. I've started building a life without you, and I don't want to go back."

"I understand that," he replied, his voice steady. "But can't we at least explore it? I mean, you owe it to yourself to see if there's still a spark."

Priya felt torn, the old feelings swirling within her. "It's not that simple. I'm seeing someone else, someone who's been there for me."

Rishi leaned in closer, searching her eyes. "Aarav, right? I get it. He seems great. But I just need you to consider—what if he's not the one who makes you feel truly alive?"

She hesitated, caught in a web of conflicting emotions. "I don't know what I want anymore, Rishi. I'm confused."

"Take your time to figure it out," Rishi said gently. "But I'm here for you, whenever you're ready."

As Priya walked away from their meeting, she felt a wave of uncertainty wash over her. Could she truly revisit a relationship with Rishi? Or had she found something special with Aarav that she couldn't let go of?

Back at home, she poured her thoughts into her journal, trying to make sense of it all. Writing had always been her refuge, and as the words flowed, she felt a semblance of clarity.

That evening, she received a call from Aarav.

"Hey! How was your day?" he asked, his voice cheerful.

"It was okay," she replied, forcing a smile. "I met Rishi."

"Really?" Aarav sounded surprised. "How did that go?"

"We talked," she said cautiously. "He wants to make amends."

"Did you tell him about us?" Aarav asked, his tone shifting slightly.

"I did, but I think he's still hoping for something more," she admitted.

Aarav sighed, and Priya could sense the weight of the situation between them. "I want you to be happy, Priya. But I also want you to be honest with yourself. What do you really want?"

"I wish I knew," she confessed, tears stinging her eyes. "I care about you so much, Aarav. But Rishi has a history with me that's hard to shake off."

"We'll figure it out together, whatever it is," Aarav replied softly. "Just be open with me."

That night, Priya lay awake, her heart heavy with uncertainty. She felt as if she were at a crossroads, with two paths stretching before her—one leading back to the familiarity of her past with Rishi, and the other leading to the uncertain future with Aarav.

12

A New Light

As the days passed, Priya found herself increasingly preoccupied with the decision she faced. Rishi had become a constant presence in her thoughts, and every time she met Aarav, she felt the guilt gnawing at her. She wanted to be honest, but how could she convey the complexity of her emotions without hurting him?

On a rainy afternoon, Priya met Aarav at their favorite café. The rhythmic sound of rain against the window created a cozy atmosphere, but Priya's heart felt anything but warm. She fidgeted with her coffee cup, knowing that she had to speak up.

"Aarav, I've been doing a lot of thinking," she began, her voice trembling slightly.

"About Rishi?" he asked, his expression serious.

"Yes," she replied, swallowing hard. "I think we need to talk about him more directly."

He nodded, encouraging her to continue.

"I appreciate everything you've done for me, and I care about you so much," Priya said, her heart racing. "But Rishi has brought up so many feelings I thought I had put to rest. I don't want to hurt you, but I also can't ignore the past."

Aarav leaned back in his chair, processing her words. “I understand that. It’s not easy to let go of someone you’ve shared so much history with. But where does that leave us?”

Priya felt a surge of emotion. “I’m scared, Aarav. Scared of losing you, scared of going back to Rishi. I don’t want to break your heart, but I also don’t want to make a choice out of fear.”

“I don’t want you to choose me out of obligation either,” Aarav said, his voice steady. “You need to be true to yourself.”

Tears filled Priya’s eyes as she tried to hold back the flood of emotions. “I wish I could see the future. I wish I knew what to do.”

Aarav reached across the table, taking her hand gently. “Whatever happens, just remember that I’m here for you. You deserve to explore your feelings, even if it leads you away from me.”

His words struck her deeply, filling her with both gratitude and sorrow. “I don’t want to hurt you, Aarav. You mean so much to me.”

“And you mean the world to me,” he replied, squeezing her hand. “But I also want you to be happy, even if it means letting you go.”

That evening, as Priya walked home through the rain, she felt the weight of her decision pressing down on her. The past and present collided within her, leaving her dizzy with uncertainty.

Back in her apartment, she opened her journal and began to write. With each stroke of the pen, she poured her heart onto the page, trying to untangle the web of emotions that bound her. She knew she had to confront her feelings—no matter how painful it might be.

In the quiet of her room, Priya finally closed her eyes and made a choice. It was time to face the truth, both with herself and with Aarav. She couldn't continue living in a state of limbo; she needed clarity, and that meant confronting Rishi once more.

13

Unwritten Chapter

The next morning, Priya awoke with a determination she hadn't felt in weeks. The rain from the previous night had washed the world clean, and as the sun peeked through her curtains, it illuminated her thoughts like a spotlight. She knew she needed to confront Rishi again, to lay bare the tangled emotions that had been clouding her mind.

After breakfast, she picked up her phone, her fingers trembling slightly as she typed a message to Rishi. *Can we meet today? I think we need to talk.*

To her surprise, he replied almost instantly. *Sure! How about that café on Maple Street at 2 PM?*

Priya's heart raced as she read the message. This was it. She had to be honest, not just with Rishi but with herself as well. She spent the morning preparing mentally, practicing what she would say in front of the mirror. The anxiety churned in her stomach, but with every affirmation she spoke, she felt a bit more grounded.

When she arrived at the café, Rishi was already there, sitting at a table by the window, looking out at the bustling street. The sight of him stirred up a mix of nostalgia and apprehension within her. He turned as she approached, a smile spreading across his face that faded slightly when he noticed the seriousness in her eyes.

"Hey, Priya," he said, gesturing for her to sit down. "I'm glad you came."

"Thanks for meeting me, Rishi," she replied, her voice steady despite the fluttering in her chest. "I've been doing a lot of thinking since our last conversation."

Rishi nodded, his expression encouraging. "I've been thinking too. I really want to make things right between us."

Taking a deep breath, Priya decided to be upfront. "I appreciate that, but I need to be honest. I've started seeing someone else—Aarav. He's been incredibly supportive, and I care about him deeply."

Rishi's expression shifted from hopeful to conflicted. "I see. That makes things a bit more complicated."

"I know," Priya said, her heart sinking. "But I think I need to explore my feelings for Aarav without any distractions. I don't want to keep coming back to you, hoping for something that might not happen."

Rishi leaned back, his fingers tapping nervously on the table. "I understand. But I also want you to know that I still care about you. You're important to me."

"I care about you too, Rishi," she said, her voice softening. "But the past we had—it was filled with so much uncertainty. I don't want to slip back into those old patterns."

"I've changed, Priya. I've done a lot of soul-searching since we broke up. I realize now how much I took you for granted. I don't want to lose you again," he replied earnestly.

Priya felt a pang in her chest at his words. "I need to focus on myself right now. I need to figure out what I want and who I want to be. I can't keep living in a state of confusion."

Silence hung between them, filled only by the soft clinking of cups and murmurs from other patrons. Finally, Rishi spoke again, his tone somber. “If you feel this way, I won’t stand in your way. But I’ll always be here if you need to talk.”

Priya nodded, feeling the weight of finality in his words. “Thank you for understanding. I truly wish you the best.”

As she left the café, Priya felt a mixture of relief and sorrow. She had confronted her past, but it didn’t mean that it was easy to let go. The memories lingered like shadows, and she hoped that this was the step she needed to move forward.

That evening, Priya texted Aarav, asking if he wanted to meet up. She felt a sudden urgency to reconnect with him, to bridge the emotional gap that had formed since their last conversation. Aarav replied enthusiastically, and they arranged to meet at a local park.

14

Photographs of Yesterday

The park was alive with the sounds of laughter and rustling leaves as Priya arrived. The sun was setting, casting a golden glow over everything, and she felt a sense of calm wash over her. Aarav was already there, leaning against a tree, a book in his hands. He looked up as she approached, his face lighting up with a smile that made her heart flutter.

"Hey! You look radiant," he said, closing his book and stepping forward to embrace her. The warmth of his hug enveloped her, making her feel safe.

"Thanks," she replied, feeling a rush of gratitude. "I've missed this."

"Me too," Aarav said, pulling away slightly to look into her eyes. "I've been thinking about our conversation. How are you holding up?"

Priya hesitated for a moment, feeling the weight of her earlier discussions with Rishi. "I had a conversation with Rishi today," she began, trying to gauge Aarav's reaction.

Aarav's expression became serious. "And?"

"I told him about us. I think it's time for me to truly move on from my past," she said, her voice steady. "I want to focus on what we have."

Relief washed over Aarav's face, and he took her hands in his. "That's great to hear, Priya. I want you to know that I'm here for you, no matter what. I care about you deeply."

Her heart swelled at his words. "I care about you too, Aarav. You've been my rock during all this confusion, and I want to explore where this connection can take us."

They sat on a nearby bench, the evening breeze whispering around them. Priya could feel the shift in their dynamic, a renewed sense of intimacy blossoming between them.

"What do you want from this?" Aarav asked, his eyes searching hers. "I mean, moving forward. I want to know what you really desire."

Priya took a deep breath, contemplating her answer. "I want to build something real with you. I want to explore this connection and see where it leads. I want us to create our own story."

Aarav's expression softened, a smile breaking through the seriousness. "I would love that. Let's take things one step at a time. No pressure, just us figuring things out together."

"I'd like that," Priya said, feeling a sense of hope bloom within her. "I feel lighter just saying it."

As the sun dipped below the horizon, casting a fiery glow across the sky, Priya felt as if a new chapter was beginning—one filled with promise and excitement. For the first time in weeks, she felt a sense of clarity, as if the clouds that had shadowed her heart were finally parting.

They talked about their dreams, their favorite memories, and the little things that brought them joy. Laughter mingled with the sweet sounds of the park, and Priya realized how easy it was to be with Aarav. He listened intently, his gaze unwavering, and she felt seen in a way she hadn't for a long time.

As the evening drew to a close, Aarav walked her home, their hands intertwined. Priya felt a rush of warmth coursing through her, a sense of belonging that she had longed for. When they reached her doorstep, Aarav leaned in closer, his eyes sparkling.

"Can I kiss you?" he asked, his voice low and sincere.

"Yes," Priya breathed, her heart racing.

As their lips met, the world around them faded away, leaving only the two of them in that moment. It was soft, tentative, and full of promise—a kiss that felt like the beginning of something beautiful.

When they finally pulled away, Aarav's expression was filled with joy and a hint of disbelief. "Wow," he said, a grin breaking across his face. "I've been waiting for that."

"Me too," Priya admitted, feeling a giddy rush of happiness.

As she stepped inside her apartment, she leaned against the door, a smile playing on her lips. She had faced her past, made difficult choices, and taken steps toward a new future. And for the first time in a long time, she felt excited about what was to come.

15

Healing

The days turned into weeks, and Priya and Aarav's relationship blossomed. Their conversations deepened, filled with laughter and dreams for the future. Aarav encouraged Priya's writing, often asking her to share her work, and she felt her creativity reignite. For the first time in a long time, she found joy in expressing herself through her words.

However, as the initial thrill of their romance settled into a comfortable routine, Priya felt a familiar unease creeping back into her mind. The echoes of her past with Rishi lingered like shadows, and although she was determined to focus on Aarav, she couldn't shake the feeling that unresolved issues still loomed over her.

One evening, while they were sitting on the couch, sharing a bottle of wine and watching a movie, Aarav turned to her, a curious expression on his face. "You've been a bit distant lately. Is everything okay?"

Priya hesitated, her heart racing. She didn't want to burden him with her insecurities, but the honesty of their relationship required transparency. "I think I'm just still processing everything from my past. It's hard to shake off old habits."

Aarav nodded, his gaze earnest. "I understand. It's normal to have lingering feelings after a breakup. I just want you to know that I'm here for you. You can talk to me about anything."

His sincerity warmed her heart, and she felt a weight lift slightly. "I appreciate that, Aarav. It's just... I still think about Rishi sometimes, and it makes me feel guilty. I don't want that to affect us."

Aarav's expression softened. "You're not responsible for how someone else feels, Priya. You deserve to explore what makes you happy, and that includes your past. Just remember, I'm not Rishi. We're building something new, and I want to support you through this."

His words were like a balm to her worries, but Priya knew she had to confront her feelings head-on. "You're right. I just need to find a way to let go of the guilt and embrace what we have."

As the weeks progressed, Aarav continued to support her writing endeavors, encouraging her to participate in a local writers' workshop. Nervous yet excited, Priya signed up, feeling a sense of accomplishment as she took this step toward nurturing her passion.

The workshop was held in a cozy bookstore downtown, and as she walked in on the first day, she felt a mix of excitement and anxiety. The room was filled with fellow writers, each sharing their stories and experiences. Priya's heart raced as she introduced herself, but the supportive environment made her feel welcome.

After a few sessions, Priya started sharing her work with the group, including snippets about her journey with Rishi and her blossoming relationship with Aarav. The feedback she received was overwhelmingly positive, and it ignited a spark within her that she hadn't felt in ages. The more she wrote, the more she healed.

But with every step forward, the echoes of her past threatened to resurface. One evening, while reviewing her notes at home, she stumbled upon an old photo of Rishi. It was a candid shot of them laughing during a picnic, a reminder of the good times they had shared. Emotions swelled within her, and she couldn't help but wonder if she had truly moved on.

Feeling restless, she texted Aarav, inviting him to join her for a late-night walk in the park. He agreed, and soon they found themselves under a starlit sky, the air crisp with the promise of autumn.

As they strolled hand in hand, Priya felt the tension of her thoughts release slightly. "I wanted to talk to you about something," she began, her voice hesitant.

"What's on your mind?" Aarav asked, turning to face her.

"I found an old photo of Rishi today. It made me realize that while I'm excited about us, I still have unresolved feelings about the past. I don't want to keep anything from you."

Aarav stopped walking, taking a moment to absorb her words. "It's okay to have those feelings, Priya. What matters is that you're with me now. I want to understand what you're feeling."

Taking a deep breath, Priya continued, "I think I'm just scared of losing you, especially when I still think about my past. It's like I'm caught in between."

Aarav took her hands, looking deeply into her eyes. "You're not going to lose me. But you have to let me in. Talk to me when you're feeling this way. We'll figure it out together."

Priya felt a surge of gratitude. “Thank you, Aarav. Your support means everything to me. I want to be completely open with you.”

As they resumed their walk, the weight on her shoulders felt lighter. She realized that love required trust, not just in the other person but in herself as well. She was ready to let go of the past and embrace her new beginning with Aarav.

16

Destinies

Days turned into weeks, and Priya's writing flourished. She poured her heart into her work, each word a cathartic release of her emotions. The workshop provided her with a sense of community, and she cherished the friendships she was forming with fellow writers. Aarav was always there to cheer her on, attending her readings and encouraging her to share her voice.

However, just as she was settling into this new rhythm, Rishi reached out again. It started with a simple text: *Hey, can we talk? I've been thinking about everything and would love to catch up.*

Priya's heart raced at the message. Part of her wanted to ignore it, to keep moving forward with Aarav, but another part of her felt compelled to respond. After much contemplation, she replied: *Sure, let's meet.*

They agreed to meet at the same café where they had last talked, a place filled with bittersweet memories. As she walked in, the familiar scent of coffee wafted through the air, and she felt a whirlwind of emotions. Rishi was already there, seated at their old table, looking both nervous and hopeful.

"Hey," he said, offering a tentative smile as she approached. "Thanks for meeting me."

"Of course," Priya replied, trying to keep her tone neutral. "What's on your mind?"

"I've been doing a lot of thinking since we last spoke," Rishi began, his eyes earnest. "I realize now how much I miss our friendship. I've been working on myself, and I genuinely want to be in your life again, even if it's just as friends."

Priya felt a knot in her stomach. "I appreciate that, Rishi, but things are different now. I'm with Aarav, and I'm really happy with him."

Rishi's expression shifted, a hint of disappointment crossing his features. "I understand, and I'm glad you found someone who makes you happy. But I miss you, Priya. I miss us."

The weight of his words hung in the air, and Priya felt torn. She cared for Rishi but knew that allowing him back into her life could complicate things with Aarav. "I think it's best if we both focus on our new paths," she said gently. "I need to move forward, and I hope you can understand that."

"Yeah, I get it. I just wanted you to know that I'm here if you ever want to talk or if you need anything," Rishi replied, his tone somber.

As they finished their conversation, Priya felt a sense of closure wash over her. She had confronted her past, set boundaries, and acknowledged the changes in her life. However, as she left the café, doubt lingered in her mind. Had she made the right choice?

That evening, she met Aarav at their favorite park. He greeted her with his usual warm smile, and they sat together on a bench, watching the sunset. As the sky transformed into hues of orange and pink, Priya felt a sense of peace settle within her.

"Hey, how did it go with Rishi?" Aarav asked, sensing the change in her demeanor.

"I told him that I'm happy with you, and I want to focus on what we have," Priya replied, her voice steady. "But I still felt a little conflicted."

Aarav took her hand, his grip reassuring. "It's natural to feel that way, especially when you've shared a part of your life with someone for so long. But remember, you're choosing to be with me now."

"I know," she said, looking into his eyes. "I want to be with you. I just need to trust myself and this decision."

"You can do this, Priya. I believe in you," he encouraged. "And I'm here every step of the way."

As they watched the sun dip below the horizon, Priya felt a sense of resolve building within her. She was ready to embrace her future with Aarav, even if it meant confronting her past. The journey ahead would be filled with challenges, but for the first time in a long time, she felt hopeful.

17

Past Pieces

As the leaves began to turn golden with the onset of autumn, Priya's life was filled with new beginnings. Her writing had blossomed, and she felt a renewed sense of purpose. The workshop provided a sanctuary where she could express herself freely, and the feedback from her peers ignited a fire within her. Every word she wrote brought her closer to healing.

However, just as everything seemed to be falling into place, a shadow loomed on the horizon. One evening, as Priya was preparing for her first public reading, she received an unexpected call from Rishi. Her heart sank at the sight of his name flashing on her phone.

Gathering her thoughts, she answered, trying to keep her voice steady. "Hey, Rishi. What's up?"

"I know this is sudden, but I've been given an opportunity to speak at a conference in the city next month. I wanted to ask if you'd be willing to come and support me," he said, his tone a mix of hope and uncertainty.

Priya felt a whirlwind of emotions. Rishi had always been a part of her life, and the idea of attending an event where he would be presenting stirred old feelings. "I... I'll think about it," she replied, her voice wavering.

After hanging up, she felt conflicted. On one hand, she wanted to support Rishi and honor their past, but on the other, she feared that attending the conference would complicate her budding relationship with Aarav.

Later that evening, Priya met Aarav at their favorite café, eager to share her news. As they settled into a cozy corner with steaming mugs of coffee, she took a deep breath. "Rishi called me today. He's speaking at a conference next month and wants me to come support him."

Aarav's expression shifted slightly, concern etched on his features. "And how do you feel about that?"

"I'm not sure," Priya admitted, her brow furrowing. "Part of me wants to go for the support, but another part of me is worried about how it might affect us."

Aarav leaned in, his gaze steady. "I want you to do what feels right for you. But you also have to consider how it might impact our relationship. I trust you, but I need to know you're being honest with yourself."

Priya felt a lump form in her throat. "I don't want to hurt you, Aarav. You've been amazing, and I don't want to jeopardize what we have."

"You're not jeopardizing anything by wanting to support someone who was once important in your life," Aarav said gently. "But if you decide to go, you need to be open about your feelings and what it means for us."

As they talked, Priya realized that her relationship with Aarav had grown stronger, built on trust and understanding. "I'll think it over and let you know my decision," she promised, feeling grateful for his support.

Over the next few days, Priya weighed her options. She found herself immersed in writing, using her thoughts about Rishi and her feelings for Aarav as inspiration for her next piece. Yet, the decision loomed heavily over her, leaving her restless and distracted.

Finally, after several sleepless nights, Priya made her decision. She would attend the conference. It was important to her to support Rishi, but she knew she had to be clear about her boundaries. That evening, she texted Rishi, confirming her attendance.

As the date of the conference approached, Priya's excitement was tinged with anxiety. She confided in Aarav about her decision, and while he was supportive, she could sense his apprehension.

"Just remember, I'm here for you," he said, squeezing her hand. "You're not alone in this."

On the day of the conference, Priya felt a mix of emotions. The venue was filled with energy, and she was eager to see Rishi succeed. As she spotted him in the crowd, her heart raced. He looked sharp in his blazer, exuding confidence, and for a moment, the memories of their past flooded back.

"Priya!" Rishi exclaimed, his face lighting up as he approached her. "I'm so glad you came."

"I wouldn't miss it," she replied, forcing a smile. "You're going to do great."

As the conference progressed, Priya found herself torn between nostalgia and the reality of her current life with Aarav. Rishi's presentation was impressive, showcasing his growth and determination, and she felt a swell of pride for him.

But as the event continued, Priya's thoughts drifted to Aarav. She missed him and felt a sense of urgency to communicate her love for him. She couldn't let Rishi's presence overshadow the new life she was building.

After Rishi finished his presentation, he approached her with a triumphant smile. "What did you think? Did I do okay?"

"You were fantastic!" Priya replied genuinely. "I'm really proud of you."

"Thank you for coming," Rishi said, his eyes searching hers. "It means a lot to me."

Feeling a twinge of guilt, Priya decided to address the elephant in the room. "Rishi, I want you to know that I'm in a relationship with someone who makes me really happy. I hope we can support each other as friends moving forward."

Rishi's expression softened, but she could see a flicker of disappointment in his eyes. "I get it. I just didn't realize how much I missed you until today."

"I miss our friendship too, but I can't go back to what we had. I need to be honest with myself," Priya replied, her heart racing.

Rishi nodded, a sad smile crossing his face. "I respect that, Priya. I really do."

As they parted ways, Priya felt a sense of relief mixed with sadness. She had faced her past, set boundaries, and remained true to herself. The conference had been a turning point, and now it was time to focus on her future with Aarav.

Later that evening, as she returned home, Priya couldn't shake the feeling of longing for Aarav. She quickly texted him, hoping to meet for dinner. When he arrived, she could see the concern in his eyes.

"Hey, how did it go?" he asked, his tone cautious.

"Rishi did great, and I told him about us. It felt good to be honest," Priya replied, her heart swelling with emotion.

Aarav's expression softened. "I'm proud of you, Priya. You handled it with grace."

"I missed you so much today," she confessed, wrapping her arms around him. "Being there made me realize how important you are to me."

As they held each other, Priya felt a warmth spread through her. She was ready to embrace this new chapter with Aarav, confident in their love.

18

Unheard Confessions

With the conference behind her, Priya returned to her routine, but the experience left her feeling invigorated. She dove back into her writing with renewed passion, often spending hours at the café where she and Aarav first met. The words flowed effortlessly, each page filled with her emotions and reflections on love, loss, and new beginnings.

As autumn settled into winter, the landscape transformed into a picturesque scene of falling leaves and chilly evenings. Aarav continued to be a steadfast presence in her life, his support unwavering. They spent cozy nights wrapped in blankets, watching movies or cooking together, and Priya found comfort in his laughter and warmth.

One weekend, as they walked through a local arts festival, Priya spotted an open mic booth. "I should try reading something here!" she exclaimed, excitement bubbling within her.

Aarav's eyes lit up. "Absolutely! You've been working hard, and this is the perfect opportunity to share your talent."

With a racing heart, Priya approached the booth, signed up, and nervously awaited her turn. As she stood in line, she felt Aarav's reassuring presence behind her. "You've got this, Priya. Just be yourself," he whispered, giving her a gentle nudge.

When her name was called, Priya took a deep breath and stepped onto the small stage. The crowd was warm and welcoming, and she could see Aarav smiling at her from the front row. As she began to read her piece, she poured her heart into each word, sharing her journey of love, loss, and self-discovery.

The audience listened intently, and with every line, she felt more connected to her words. The applause at the end was thunderous, and Priya's heart swelled with joy. As she stepped off the stage, Aarav enveloped her in a tight hug, pride shining in his eyes.

"You were amazing, Priya! I knew you could do it!" he cheered, his enthusiasm infectious.

"Thank you for believing in me," she said, her heart racing from the thrill of performing. "I couldn't have done it without your support."

As they wandered through the festival, hand in hand, Priya felt a sense of belonging she hadn't experienced in a long time. The connection she had with Aarav deepened, transcending their initial romantic feelings into something more profound.

Later that night, as they cuddled on the couch, Priya turned to Aarav, her voice barely above a whisper. "Can I ask you something?"

"Of course," he replied, brushing a strand of hair behind her ear.

"What do you see for us in the future?" she asked, her heart pounding.

Aarav paused, his expression thoughtful. "Honestly, I see us continuing to grow together. I want to support your dreams and be there for you, no matter what. You mean so much to me, Priya."

A wave of emotion washed over her. "You've changed my life for the better, Aarav. I want to build something real with you, something lasting."

Aarav smiled, his eyes sparkling with affection. "I want that too. You inspire me every day, and I can't wait to see where our journey takes us."

They shared a tender kiss, sealing their promise to each other. As Priya lay in Aarav's arms, she felt safe and cherished. The road ahead was uncertain, but with Aarav by her side, she knew they could face anything together.

As the winter months rolled on, their bond continued to grow stronger. They traveled to art galleries, attended poetry readings, and explored new coffee shops, savoring each moment they spent together. Aarav often surprised Priya with thoughtful gestures—little notes tucked into her bag, spontaneous dates, and encouraging words that fueled her creativity.

One evening, as they sat beneath a blanket of stars, Priya opened up about her past struggles. "I was so lost before I met you, Aarav. It's like I was living in a fog, and now everything feels vibrant and alive," she confessed, her voice tinged with vulnerability.

"You deserve all the happiness in the world, Priya. I'm just glad I get to be a part of your journey," Aarav replied, his sincerity washing over her like a warm embrace.

In that moment, Priya knew she had found her soulmate. Their love was built on trust, understanding, and mutual respect, and she cherished every moment they spent together.

But as the winter holidays approached, Priya sensed a shift in the air. An unexpected opportunity arose when she was invited to contribute to a literary magazine, and her excitement was palpable. However, she also felt a flicker of doubt. Would this newfound success draw her away from Aarav? Could she maintain the delicate balance between her career and their relationship?

As she contemplated these questions, Priya realized that communication would be key. She needed to be open with Aarav about her ambitions and the potential challenges they might face. With a deep breath, she decided to broach the subject during their next cozy evening together.

19

Love Redesigned

As the winter holidays approached, Priya found herself torn between excitement and anxiety. The opportunity to contribute to the literary magazine was a dream come true, but it also meant diving headfirst into a demanding project that could take her away from her time with Aarav.

One cozy evening, as they snuggled on the couch, Priya decided it was time to share her thoughts. The warm glow of the fireplace created an intimate atmosphere, making it the perfect setting for a serious conversation.

"Aarav," she began, her heart racing slightly, "there's something important I need to talk to you about."

He looked up from the book he was reading, concern flashing in his eyes. "What's on your mind?"

"I was invited to write for a literary magazine," she announced, her voice laced with excitement. "It's an incredible opportunity, but I'm worried about how it might affect us. I'll need to dedicate a lot of time to writing and meeting deadlines."

Aarav smiled, his pride evident. "Priya, that's amazing! I'm so happy for you. You deserve this."

"But..." she hesitated, searching for the right words. "I'm concerned that I might get so wrapped up in this project that I won't have enough time for us. I don't want to lose what we have."

Aarav reached for her hand, squeezing it gently. "You won't lose me. I want you to pursue your dreams, and I'll be here cheering you on. But we need to communicate openly about how we can make this work."

Priya felt a wave of relief wash over her. "Thank you for understanding. I just want to make sure we're both on the same page."

"I think we can find a balance. Just remember to carve out time for us amidst all the writing. We can even have writing dates together," he suggested with a wink.

She chuckled at the idea. "That sounds perfect! I'd love that."

With their hearts aligned, Priya dove into her writing project with vigor. The thrill of crafting her piece consumed her, and she spent hours at the café, pouring her soul onto the pages. Aarav remained her biggest supporter, frequently dropping by to check in on her progress, always bringing her favorite coffee or a small treat to keep her spirits high.

However, as the weeks flew by, Priya found herself becoming increasingly absorbed in her writing. She worked late into the night, and sometimes, her focus on the project led her to unintentionally neglect their time together.

One evening, Aarav came home to find Priya still hunched over her laptop, her eyes weary from staring at the screen for too long. He approached her, concern etched on his face. "Hey, you've been working really hard. Why don't we take a break and have dinner together?"

"I'm so close to finishing this section," Priya replied, not looking up. "Just give me a few more minutes."

Aarav sighed, taking a seat beside her. "I understand that it's important to you, but you also need to take care of yourself. I miss spending time with you."

Her heart sank at the sadness in his voice. Priya finally looked up, guilt washing over her. "You're right. I'm sorry, Aarav. I didn't mean to shut you out. I got carried away."

He smiled softly, though it didn't quite reach his eyes. "I want you to succeed, Priya, but I also want us to succeed. We're a team, remember?"

She nodded, feeling the weight of her neglect. "You're absolutely right. Let's have dinner together and I'll make it up to you."

As they sat at the dinner table, sharing stories and laughter, Priya realized how important it was to nurture their connection. She made a promise to herself to prioritize their time together, even amidst her busy schedule.

The next week, Priya submitted her piece to the magazine, feeling a mix of exhilaration and relief. She had poured her heart into it, and now it was out in the world. With the submission behind her, she turned her focus back to Aarav, determined to rekindle their romance.

"Let's plan a weekend getaway," she suggested one evening, her eyes sparkling with enthusiasm. "Just the two of us, away from everything."

Aarav's face lit up. "That sounds incredible! Where do you want to go?"

"I was thinking we could head to that cabin by the lake. It'll be cozy, and we can enjoy nature together," she proposed, feeling a sense of excitement bubbling within her.

"I love that idea. Let's book it!" he replied, his enthusiasm contagious.

As they made plans, Priya felt a renewed sense of hope for their relationship. She was committed to finding the right balance between her ambitions and their love.

20

Weight of Forgiveness

The following weekend arrived, and Priya was buzzing with anticipation. They packed their bags and set off for the cabin, the crisp air invigorating and filled with the scent of pine. As they drove through winding roads lined with trees, Priya felt a sense of freedom wash over her.

When they arrived, the cabin was a charming retreat nestled in the woods, complete with a beautiful view of the lake. They unloaded their bags and settled in, the warmth of the fireplace creating a cozy atmosphere.

Aarav wrapped his arms around Priya as they stood on the porch, taking in the stunning scenery. "This is perfect," he said, his voice filled with awe.

"I'm so glad you like it," Priya replied, leaning into him. "I needed this time away with you."

That evening, they cooked dinner together, laughing as they prepared a simple meal. The kitchen was filled with the aroma of garlic and herbs, and Priya felt a sense of contentment as she watched Aarav chop vegetables.

After dinner, they curled up on the couch, wrapped in blankets, and watched the stars twinkle through the cabin window. The stillness of the night enveloped them, and

Priya felt a deep sense of peace.

"I've missed this—just being together without distractions," Aarav said, looking into her eyes. "It's nice to take a break from everything."

"Me too," Priya replied, her heart swelling with affection. "I want to make more time for us, even when life gets busy."

Aarav smiled, leaning in closer. "I appreciate that. You know I'll always support you, but I need you to promise that we'll keep communicating."

"I promise," she said earnestly. "This weekend is a reminder of how important we are to each other."

As the night wore on, they shared stories, dreams, and laughter, feeling more connected than ever. The love between them had deepened, and Priya realized how lucky she was to have Aarav in her life.

The next day, they explored the surrounding woods, taking long walks hand in hand, collecting leaves and pinecones along the way. They laughed as they stumbled upon a hidden clearing, where they spread out a blanket and enjoyed a picnic lunch under the sun.

Later that afternoon, they rented a canoe and paddled across the serene lake, the water reflecting the vibrant autumn colors around them. Priya felt a rush of joy as they glided over the surface, the world around them melting away.

"This is amazing," she exclaimed, glancing at Aarav. "I can't remember the last time I felt so free."

"It's beautiful, just like you," he said, his gaze warm and sincere.

Priya's cheeks flushed at his compliment, and she leaned in to steal a quick kiss. "You always know how to make me smile."

As they returned to the cabin that evening, Priya felt a sense of fulfillment. This weekend had been exactly what she needed—a reminder of the love they shared and the importance of nurturing that bond.

As night fell, they gathered around the fireplace, sharing their dreams and aspirations. Priya opened up about her ambitions, her desire to keep writing, and her hopes for the future.

"I want to inspire others with my words," she said passionately. "And I want to do it with you by my side."

Aarav nodded, his eyes gleaming with encouragement. "You will, Priya. You have a gift, and I can't wait to see where it takes you."

As they settled down for the night, wrapped in each other's arms, Priya felt an overwhelming sense of gratitude. She had faced her past, embraced her future, and found love in Aarav—someone who truly understood her.

21

Page Turnover

After their rejuvenating weekend retreat, Priya returned to the city with renewed energy and inspiration for her writing. However, just as she was settling back into her routine, she received a surprising phone call that would test her commitment to both her career and her relationship.

"Hi, Priya! It's Sarah from the magazine," her editor's voice chirped through the phone. "We loved your piece, and we'd like to feature it in our next issue! But we need a follow-up article—something fresh and engaging. Are you interested?"

Priya's heart raced at the news. This was exactly what she had hoped for, but it also meant she would have to commit more time to writing, which could strain her time with Aarav. "Absolutely, Sarah! I'd love to contribute. What topic are you thinking about?"

"We want you to write about the writing process—how to stay motivated and overcome writer's block. It's a theme we believe resonates with many aspiring authors," Sarah explained.

"Sounds great! I'll get started right away," Priya replied, excitement bubbling within her. After hanging up, she couldn't help but feel both exhilarated and overwhelmed. She had a chance to solidify her place in the literary world, but it also meant more late nights and less time with Aarav.

That evening, Priya shared the news with Aarav while they enjoyed dinner together. His expression brightened with genuine happiness as she recounted the details of her conversation.

"That's fantastic, Priya! You've worked hard for this opportunity," he said, his pride evident.

"Thanks! I'm excited, but... I'm worried about how it will affect us. I don't want to lose the connection we've built," she admitted, her anxiety creeping in.

Aarav reached for her hand. "We'll make it work, I promise. Communication is key. Let's set specific times for our date nights so you can focus on your writing without feeling guilty."

"I appreciate that, Aarav. I'll do my best to balance it all," Priya replied, feeling reassured by his support.

However, as the days passed, Priya found herself consumed by her writing. Late nights turned into early mornings, and she became increasingly distant from Aarav. Although he was understanding, Priya could see the concern growing in his eyes.

One night, after another long day, she returned home to find Aarav waiting for her. He had made dinner, the table set with candles and a beautiful bouquet of flowers.

"Wow, this looks amazing," she said, her heart swelling with affection.

"I wanted to surprise you," he replied, his voice soft. "But I've also been worried. You've been so busy with your writing that we haven't had much time together. I miss you, Priya."

Her heart sank at the realization. “I miss you too. I’m so sorry for not making more time. I’ve just been so focused on this article, but it’s not an excuse.”

Aarav smiled gently. “I understand how important this is to you, but you need to take care of yourself too. Remember, I’m here for you. We can work on this together.”

With his words resonating in her heart, Priya knew she had to find a better balance. “You’re right. I want to make this work, for both of us. Let’s schedule our time together more intentionally.”

“Great idea. How about a writing date tomorrow? You can write, and I’ll work on my photography. We’ll still be together,” Aarav suggested, his eyes twinkling.

“I love that!” she exclaimed, feeling a wave of relief wash over her. “Thank you for being so understanding.”

That night, they shared a heartfelt conversation about their dreams and ambitions, reaffirming their commitment to each other. Priya realized that while her career was important, her relationship with Aarav was equally vital.

22

Redemption

As winter rolled into the city, Priya found a new rhythm in her life. The structured writing dates with Aarav helped her stay focused, and she made a conscious effort to reconnect with him during her breaks. It was refreshing to share her creative process, and she cherished the moments spent bouncing ideas off him.

One weekend, while Aarav was out photographing the snowy landscape, Priya decided to take a break from her writing. Inspired by their discussions, she picked up her notebook and began jotting down ideas for a new story—a narrative exploring the themes of love, ambition, and the struggle for balance.

When Aarav returned, he found her engrossed in her notes, her brow furrowed in concentration. “What are you working on?” he asked, setting down his camera and joining her at the table.

“I’m thinking about a new story,” she said, her eyes lighting up. “It’s about a couple navigating their careers while trying to keep their relationship strong. I want to capture the challenges and joys that come with that.”

Aarav leaned closer, intrigued. "That sounds fantastic! It's so relatable. You should definitely explore that."

"Thanks! I just want to do it justice. It feels personal, you know?" she admitted.

As they talked, Aarav encouraged her, sharing insights from his own experiences with photography and the balance he sought in his life. His support filled Priya with a newfound determination.

The following week, she completed her article for the magazine, pouring her heart into every word. After submitting it, she felt a wave of relief and excitement. But rather than resting, she decided to dive into her new story, drawing inspiration from her relationship with Aarav.

A few days later, Priya received an email from Sarah that sent her heart racing. "We loved your article, Priya! We'd like to feature it on the cover of the next issue. You're doing amazing work!"

Overjoyed, she shared the news with Aarav, who celebrated her achievement with a spontaneous dinner at their favorite restaurant. They laughed and reminisced about their journey, recognizing how far they had come both individually and as a couple.

"Do you remember when we first started dating? I was so unsure of myself, and now look at us," Priya said, her eyes sparkling with gratitude.

Aarav smiled, "We've both grown so much. You've found your voice as a writer, and I'm proud of you."

Feeling inspired, Priya leaned across the table, her heart full. "I couldn't have done it without you, Aarav. Your support has meant everything to me."

As they savored their meal, Priya realized that her love for Aarav only fueled her passion for writing. She had come to understand that it was possible to chase her dreams while nurturing their relationship, and she felt an overwhelming sense of hope for the future.

That night, as they walked home under the twinkling city lights, Priya felt an undeniable bond forming between them—a bond strengthened by understanding, communication, and love.

"I can't wait to see where our journeys take us," Aarav said, squeezing her hand.

"Neither can I," Priya replied, her heart swelling with optimism. "Together, we can achieve anything."

With a renewed sense of purpose, they entered their apartment, ready to face whatever challenges lay ahead, knowing they would always have each other's backs.

23

Forever Together

As winter began to thaw, Priya's new story took shape, filled with rich characters and the emotional complexities of love and ambition. With each word, she explored her own fears and aspirations, drawing from her experiences with Aarav. But just as she was finding her footing, a shadow from her past resurfaced.

One evening, while working at her favorite coffee shop, Priya received a text from her ex-boyfriend, Rohan. "Hey, Priya. Hope you're doing well. I'd love to catch up sometime."

Her heart sank as memories of their tumultuous relationship flooded back. Rohan had been charming but self-centered, often making her feel inadequate. She hadn't spoken to him in over a year, and the thought of reconnecting sent waves of anxiety through her.

She hesitated to tell Aarav, fearing it might spark jealousy or insecurity. But that evening, as they settled into their cozy couch with steaming mugs of tea, Priya decided to come clean. "Aarav, I received a text from Rohan today," she said, her voice trembling slightly.

Aarav's expression shifted, a mix of concern and curiosity crossing his face. "Oh? What did he want?"

"He just wants to catch up. I don't know how to feel about it," Priya confessed, biting her lip. "Part of me is curious, but another part is terrified."

"Have you thought about what you want?" Aarav asked, his tone steady but gentle.

Priya took a deep breath. "I think I've moved on. Rohan was part of my past, and I've worked so hard to build something real with you. But I don't want to hurt you either."

Aarav nodded thoughtfully. "You deserve to confront your past on your terms, Priya. But remember, I'm here for you. You can choose to meet him, but it shouldn't come at the expense of what we have."

"Thank you for understanding," Priya said, relief washing over her. "I think I need to respond, not to rekindle anything but to find closure."

The following day, Priya texted Rohan, agreeing to meet for coffee but setting clear boundaries. As the days passed, she found herself increasingly anxious about the meeting. What if Rohan tried to manipulate her emotions? What if he made her doubt her relationship with Aarav?

When the day finally arrived, Priya steeled herself as she entered the café. Rohan was already seated at a corner table, a confident smile on his face. As she approached, she felt a mix of nostalgia and apprehension.

"Hey, Priya! It's great to see you," he said, standing to greet her with a hug.

"Yeah, it's been a while," she replied, forcing a smile as they sat down.

As they chatted, Rohan talked about his life, his recent successes, and his new girlfriend. Priya listened, nodding along, but inside, she felt a growing sense of detachment.

"Do you ever miss the good times we had?" Rohan asked, leaning forward with a hint of nostalgia in his eyes.

Priya took a moment to gather her thoughts. "I think it's important to remember the lessons from the past, but I'm also focused on my present. I've built a new life, and I'm happy with it," she replied, her voice steady.

"Is it because of that guy you're with now? What's his name... Aarav?" Rohan smirked, a hint of disdain in his tone.

"Yes, Aarav. He's supportive and truly cares about me, which is something I never had with you," Priya shot back, surprising herself with her boldness.

Rohan's expression faltered, but he quickly regained his composure. "I just wanted to see if you're happy. That's all."

With a newfound clarity, Priya realized that she had nothing left to prove to Rohan. She was ready to close that chapter of her life once and for all. "I am happy, Rohan. And I don't need to revisit the past to know that."

As they wrapped up the conversation, Priya felt a weight lift off her shoulders. She had faced her fears and emerged stronger, ready to embrace the future with Aarav.

24

Love Rewritten

The sun shone brightly as spring unfolded in the city, bringing with it a sense of renewal. Priya felt lighter, her heart unburdened by her past. After her meeting with Rohan, she returned to Aarav with a sense of empowerment, eager to share her experience.

"Hey, how did it go?" Aarav asked, his eyes searching hers for reassurance.

"I'm done with the past," Priya said, a smile spreading across her face. "I told Rohan that I'm happy with you and that I've moved on. I finally feel free."

Aarav's expression brightened. "That's amazing, Priya! I'm proud of you for standing your ground. You deserve to feel that freedom."

With newfound energy, Priya dove back into her writing, pouring her experiences into her work. Her story began to take on a life of its own, resonating with the themes of love, growth, and the courage to embrace change. She submitted her manuscript to several publishers, hopeful for the opportunity to share her journey with the world.

As the weeks passed, Priya and Aarav continued to nurture their relationship. They took long walks in the park, explored new art galleries, and enjoyed quiet nights in, finding joy in each moment spent together.

One evening, as they sat on the couch watching a movie, Aarav turned to Priya, his expression serious. "I've been thinking about us a lot lately," he began, his voice steady but soft.

"Me too," Priya replied, her heart racing.

"I love you, Priya. You've brought so much joy and inspiration into my life, and I can't imagine a future without you," Aarav confessed, his gaze unwavering.

"I love you too, Aarav. You've helped me discover my strength, and I want to build a future together," Priya said, her voice filled with emotion.

Aarav reached for her hand, his thumb gently caressing her palm. "Then let's take the next step. I want us to grow together, in our careers and in our lives."

With tears of happiness in her eyes, Priya nodded. "I'd love that."

As spring blossomed around them, Priya and Aarav embraced the promise of new beginnings. They celebrated each other's achievements, supporting one another's dreams while cultivating a love that grew deeper and more profound with each passing day.

One sunny afternoon, as they walked through a vibrant flower market, Aarav paused, a thoughtful look on his face. "You know, we should plan a trip together—somewhere we can escape and explore."

"I'd love that! A writing retreat perhaps? We can find inspiration in nature," Priya suggested, her eyes sparkling.

"Perfect! We'll make it a creative getaway," Aarav replied, excitement evident in his voice.

As they picked out fresh flowers, Priya couldn't help but reflect on how far she had come. From the confusion of her past to the clarity of her present, she realized that her journey was just beginning. With Aarav by her side, she felt ready to face whatever challenges life would throw their way.

That evening, as they prepared dinner together, Aarav turned to her with a playful grin. “What do you think about making our next date night a little more adventurous?”

“Oh? What do you have in mind?” Priya asked, intrigued.

“Cooking something we’ve never tried before! Let’s challenge ourselves,” he suggested, his enthusiasm contagious.

Priya laughed, the joy bubbling inside her. “Count me in! Let’s create a masterpiece together.”

As they navigated the chaos of their kitchen, laughter filled the air, and the love between them deepened with each shared moment. Priya realized that their relationship was built on mutual support, respect, and a shared passion for life.

In that beautiful chaos, as they stirred pots and danced to music, Priya knew they were crafting not just a meal, but a life filled with love, adventure, and endless possibilities. They were writing their own story, one that was uniquely theirs, full of love and hope for the future.

After The Storm: Lessons Of Life/love

As the final pages of this story come to a close, we are left with the echoes of choices, love, and the journey that each character has undergone. Priya, Aarav, and Rishi walked through the twisted paths of their hearts, navigating the twists of relationships that their lives had for them. Love isn't always about getting what we want or even holding on to what we once had. It is about understanding ourselves, learning when to let go, and when to fight for what matters most.

Aarav's search for self, Priya's conflict between the past and present, and Rishi's comeback remind us of the complexity of human emotions and love they had for them. In the end, it wasn't about finding a perfect ending but accepting the imperfect beauty of life's journey. Every step they took, every decision they made, shaped not only their relationships but also their futures.

We've traveled with them through joy, heartbreak, misunderstandings, and realizations. Their struggles and achievements resembles our's because, at some level, they are ours too. Whether you rooted for one relationship or found yourself broke between what you thought was best for them, the story speaks to the universal truth of love: it's never simple, but it's always worth exploring **(*Happily ever after is not a fairytale, its a choice*).**

Thank you for joining these characters in their journey. The end of the book is not the end of their stories, just as it isn't the end of ours. There's always another chapter waiting to be written, and every experience shapes the pages of our lives. Whether it's through love found, love lost, or love transformed, we are all part of this ongoing narrative.

As you close this book, may you carry with you the lessons of forgiveness, hope, and the courage to move forward, even when the road is uncertain.

Hope this work excited you all.

"*Thank You,*
-Mihir Bommisetty"

www.ingramcontent.com/pod-product-compliance
Lightning Source LLC
LaVergne TN
LVHW090424210926
848480LV00002B/675